Monkey Subdues the White-Bone Demon

Adapted by
Wang Hsing-pei

Drawings by
Chao Hung-pen and Chien Hsiao-tai

Fredonia Books
Amsterdam, The Netherlands

Monkey Subdues the White-Bone Demon

Adapted by
wang Hsing-pei
Drawings by
Chao Hung-pen and Chien Hsiao-tai

ISBN: 1-58963-368-7

Copyright © 2001 by Fredonia Books

Reprinted from the 1976 edition

Fredonia Books
Amsterdam, the Netherlands
http://www.fredoniabooks.com

THIS picture-story book, "Monkey Subdues the White-Bone Demon," is based on an episode from *The Pilgrimage to the West,* a mythological novel by Wu Cheng-en. The novel has had a wide appeal among Chinese readers since its appearance in the 16th century, and its hero, Monkey, has become one of the most lovable figures in Chinese literature.

Monkey is a fearless and loyal character capable of performing supernatural feats. In defiance of the powers that be, he creates havoc in heaven, and consequently is imprisoned by Buddha under the Mountain of the Five Elements. Five hundred years later he becomes a Buddhist follower and escorts the monk Hsuan-tsang on his pilgrimage to the west to seek Buddhist scriptures. During the journey he kills demons and performs many other deeds. In the story of their encounter with the White-Bone Demon, Hsuan-tsang fails to see through the demon's disguise, and claims that even a demon can be made to mend its ways. But Monkey refuses to be taken in, and for this he is sent away by Hsuan-tsang. Only after he has saved the monk from the man-eating monster's jaws does the latter realize that people are not always what they appear to be, and that the only way to deal with a demon is resolutely to wipe it out.

The line drawings are in the traditional Chinese style, while the operatic costumes in which the characters appear add to the legendary atmosphere of the story.

The monk Hsuan-tsang, escorted by his disciples Monkey, Pigsy and Sandy, was on his way to the west in search of the Buddhist scriptures. The journey was to be a hard one, and Monkey was chosen to lead the way.

As they trekked on, the sky suddenly clouded over. Ahead they saw an ominous array of towering precipices. "Be on your guard, Brothers," warned Monkey. "I'm afraid there are demons around!"

Hsuan-tsang was so alarmed that he could not keep his seat in the saddle. Monkey helped him to dismount. "Keep calm, Master!" he said. "As long as I'm with you I'll kill any demons that cross your path." Hsuan-tsang reproached him, saying that it was a sin against Buddhism to kill.

At this moment a black cloud floated across the sky, instantly alerting Monkey. But as he leaped into the air to look closer, the cloud disappeared behind a mountain peak.

Pigsy laughed at Monkey. "Brother, you're far too suspicious," he said. Then patting his belly he added, "Let's move on and find something to eat."

But Monkey was worried. "This is a barren mountain and there's no sign of human life for miles around. I'd better go ahead to have a look and find you some fresh fruit," he said.

With his gold-inlaid staff Monkey traced a magic ring on the ground around the three, telling them to stay where they were and not to accost anybody or eat anything while he was away.

No sooner was Monkey gone than the black cloud reappeared and
hovered over the three. Riding on the cloud was the Wolf Demon
of the mountain out on patrol.

On this mountain lived the White-Bone Demon with many other demons under her command — Lion, Tiger, Bear and Wolf — all man-eating ogres. When the Wolf Demon returned to their cave with his discovery, the demons and imps clamoured for permission to go and capture Hsuan-tsang and his disciples.

The Lion King took his weapon and was about to leave with several goblins when the White-Bone Demon said with a cold laugh, "Don't you know the monk Hsuan-tsang has a disciple called Monkey?"

At the mention of Monkey the goblins paled with fright. But the
White-Bone Demon sneered, "No need to panic. I have a way to
deal with him."

The White-Bone Demon came out and saw Hsuan-tsang, Pigsy and Sandy sitting deep in meditation. Monkey was nowhere to be seen.

Congratulating herself on her luck, the White-Bone Demon was about
to fling herself upon Hsuan-tsang when golden rays shot forth from
the ring Monkey had traced on the ground. She found it impos-
sible to break into the circle.

"Monkey knows defence," she thought, "but I can change myself into another form. Then won't they fall into my trap?" And with that she disappeared behind a rock.

Quick as a wink there appeared from behind the rock a maiden with flowers in her hair and carrying steamed buns in a basket. Smiling sweetly and reciting Buddhist scriptures, she approached Hsuan-tsang and his two disciples.

Pigsy was so hungry he could not sit still. When he heard the scriptures and smelt the fragrant steamed buns, he quickly opened his eyes and got up in delighted anticipation.

Ignoring Monkey's warning, he slipped out of the ring and greeted the girl with a bow. The girl uttered a little cry as if in alarm, and ran away.

Pigsy ran after her, shouting, "What are you afraid of? I'm a priest from the Tang territory in the east." Swinging her basket, she giggled, "Don't be angry with me, venerable priest. I shouldn't have been so suspicious."

"You're not to blame," said Pigsy. "But if my Big Brother Monkey had seen you in these mountains he would have taken you for a demon." The girl told Pigsy that she lived somewhere in the west, that her parents were Buddhists and had asked her to go to the Temple of the Heavenly King to offer sacrifices.

Pigsy asked her to take him to the temple.   Hsuan-tsang hesitated to
let him go, while Sandy said Pigsy should definitely wait until Monkey
returned.

The girl gave Pigsy a wink and started off. Pigsy hurriedly pulled Hsuan-tsang out of the circle and yelled at the top of his voice, "Wait, girlie, we're coming with you!"

Sandy ran up and asked the girl outright who she was. "Master,"
she cried all in a fluster, and hid behind Hsuan-tsang.

The girl smiled when Hsuan-tsang reprimanded Sandy for his bad manners. "The Temple of the Heavenly King lies ahead," she said. "Follow me, venerable priests."

Master and disciples were being led off by the girl when they heard a shout from above, "You impudent demon!" and down jumped Monkey.

On his way back Monkey had seen the girl talking with his master and had recognized her as a demon. He rushed up and struck her with his staff.

As the girl-form sank to the ground quite lifeless, the White-Bone Demon's spirit emerged from it as a wisp of cloud, and made off. Monkey gave chase.

Hsuan-tsang was shocked and protested that it was a sin to kill.
Pigsy also reprimanded Monkey. Only Sandy defended him, saying
Monkey had a keen eye for demons and would never kill an innocent
person.

28

Hsuan-tsang was wondering who the girl was when an old woman, bamboo stick in one hand and rosary in the other, appeared from the other side of the mountain, reciting Buddhist scriptures as she hobbled along.

The old woman was the White-Bone Demon in another disguise. Pigsy was scared. "We're in for it," he cried, "this woman must be the mother of the girl and has come looking for her."

When the woman asked Pigsy if he had seen her daughter, he looked to Hsuan-tsang for help. But Hsuan-tsang simply hung his head and said nothing.

The old woman saw the girl lying on the ground. Without waiting for Pigsy's reply, she burst out crying. "Oh, my poor child," she wailed, "who would have thought a Buddhist believer would come to such a tragic end!"

She caught Pigsy by the sleeve and began reproaching him.

The monk apologized profusely. "Don't blame him," he said. "It's all the fault of my disciple Monkey. I should have been more strict with him."

The woman let go of Pigsy and said with a sigh, "This venerable priest is really compassionate. It's the will of Providence." She begged the monk to go with her to buy a coffin in a nearby village, and he went quite willingly.

As they were picking their way along a small path, they heard a peal of laughter coming from behind a big tree, and in a flash Monkey brought his staff down on the woman before she could get away.

The demon changed itself into smoke and made good its escape.
Monkey was again about to give chase when Hsuan-tsang stopped
him. "Are you crazy, that you kill both mother and daughter?"

"Master, you've been deceived," Monkey explained. "They're not mother and daughter; they're one and the same demon in disguise. Where do you think that girl came from when there are no houses for miles around here? And how could an old woman climb up this mountain path?"

"She was definitely human," said Pigsy, swinging the old woman's rosary. "Buddhism forbids killing above all," the monk said angrily. "I may forgive you, but Buddha will surely punish you."

Hsuan-tsang began to cast a spell over Monkey. If Monkey was disobedient Hsuan-tsang would order a tight metal band around his head. The pain was unbearable. Sandy begged for mercy on Monkey's behalf. "If Big Brother Monkey hadn't risked his life to protect you from the demons," he said, "they would have de-

The monk listened to Sandy's plea and recalled his spell. Monkey
wondered what to do next. If he let the demon go Hsuan-tsang
would sooner or later fall into its trap. So, saying he was going
to scout the route, he went in search of the demon.

Back in her cave after two escapes, the White-Bone Demon sat on her throne fuming. She was thinking of some way to get the better of Monkey.

Soon she came out of the cave. She had an idea. She changed some trees by the path into a thatched cottage and herself into a white-haired old man sitting beside it.

Monkey saw the old man and knew it must be the demon. "Tricky, aren't you! Do you think you can fool me by changing into another form?" he shouted, then swept down on the demon with his staff.

The demon had been expecting the monk Hsuan-tsang and not
Monkey. Panicked by Monkey's sudden descent, he got up nimbly
to fight with his stick.

The demon's arms grew numb as he parried Monkey's blows.

The demon suddenly saw Hsuan-tsang and the others approaching, and he ran to them crying, "Help! Help!"

Falling on his knees before the monk, he begged for protection. Monkey closed in and was about to strike his final blow when Hsuan-tsang intervened.

"You treacherous disciple!" said Hsuan-tsang. "You've killed a mother and daughter and now you want to commit another sin!" The demon began howling.

"You've killed my old wife and my lovely daughter!" he cried. "I've nothing to live for. You might as well kill me too." And he rushed up to Monkey.

Monkey was enraged and shouted, "You're a demon, whatever form you take. You can't fool me!"

As Monkey raised his staff, Hsuan-tsang rushed to the demon's aid. "A Buddhist disciple must be compassionate," he pronounced. "Even if he's a demon you should persuade him to mend his ways, not kill him." But Monkey replied, "You may save *him*, Master, but he will never let *you* be."

When Monkey raised his staff again, Hsuan-tsang took hold of his arm. "Better kill *me*," he said. The demon wailed through his tears, "All you know is killing. What's the use of your charitable deeds and seeking Buddhist scriptures?"

And Hsuan-tsang started to cast his spell again, so that Monkey fell to the ground in agony.

The demon was all too pleased, while the terrified Pigsy and Sandy
pleaded for Monkey.

Hsuan-tsang stopped casting his spell and Monkey got to his feet and sprang upon the demon. Then Hsuan-tsang resumed, and Monkey was soon seized with pain again.

Still Monkey gathered all his strength and struck the demon a telling
blow. It escaped only by making a magic sign.

Monkey started giving chase when a cloud appeared in the sky and out of it floated a strip of yellow silk.

The silk fell at the feet of Hsuan-tsang, who picked it up and read:
"Buddha is compassionate and will never tolerate killing any creature.
If you keep Monkey with you, you'll never get the scriptures."

Hsuan-tsang sighed and told Monkey to return to his home on Flower
and Fruit Mountain, saying he was too undisciplined. But Monkey
replied, "This is another trick of the demon. You mustn't let your-
self be taken in. The trip to the west is difficult, with demons all
the way. I must see you through the journey."

Pigsy and Sandy also begged that Monkey be allowed to remain with them, but Hsuan-tsang turned a deaf ear to their pleas, saying it was the will of Buddha that he leave them.

So Monkey bade farewell to Pigsy and Sandy, asking them to take good care of their master on his pilgrimage.

Then, bowing before Hsuan-tsang, Monkey warned him to distin-
guish between good and evil, man and devil, and to look out for
himself. Then he set out through the clouds to return to Flower
and Fruit Mountain.

The sky darkened and a cold wind sprang up. The three pilgrims gathered up their belongings and continued on their journey, not a word passing between them.

They were thinking about finding shelter for the night when they heard the chiming of a bell from afar. Then, in front of them, appeared the red walls of a temple in a grove of trees.

Pigsy cried out in joy at the sight of the temple, and urged the monk
to hurry up. "We can worship Buddha here," said Hsuan-tsang.
Over the temple gate was a tablet inscribed with: Temple of the
Heavenly King.

The monk got down from his horse and the three entered the temple, knelt before the images and prayed to Buddha for a safe and successful journey.

Suddenly the central image opened its mouth and rasped, "It's a foolish monk that can't tell the true from the false. Seize him!" In a flash the benign-looking images had all turned into demons.

Seeing their master in the demons' clutches, Pigsy and Sandy tried to rescue him. The White-Bone Demon shrieked to her followers to surround them in a tight cordon.

The pilgrims were overpowered by the demons. Sandy was captured and Pigsy had to fight his way out.

Out in the open Pigsy looked back and what he saw was the tightly-shut stone door of a cave. The temple had vanished!

Pigsy thought about Monkey's parting advice, and he was ashamed and worried. As a last resort, he got on his magic cloud and rode off to Flower and Fruit Mountain to ask for Monkey's help.

Outside Water Curtain Cave on the mountain, Pigsy's way was blocked by a host of little monkeys. They told Pigsy that their king had been too unhappy recently to receive guests.

Pigsy introduced himself, then told them he had come in an emergency. One of the little monkeys told Pigsy that their king was always thinking of Hsuan-tsang and the others, and bade him wait while he went in to tell Monkey.

When their king had returned, the little monkeys were delighted. But Monkey remained in low spirits, always worrying about his master. Now, when he learned of Pigsy's arrival, he told the little monkeys to show the guest in at once.

Pigsy stumped in with such a gloomy look that Monkey knew something was wrong. Pigsy told his story and begged Monkey to go with him and rescue their master.

Monkey jumped up, but then sat down again. "Why worry!" he laughed. "Master's kindheartedness will persuade the demon to set him free."

Nonplussed, Pigsy begged Monkey, at the same time blaming their master for being so unwise as to send Monkey away. But Monkey remained in his seat as though totally indifferent.

Pigsy slapped his chest, screaming, "You've lost all sense of right-
eousness. I'm no coward, I'll go and fight the demon to the last!"
With this, Pigsy went off in a huff.

The moment Pigsy was gone, Monkey took off his robe and crown, ready to go into battle. The little monkeys were puzzled.

Monkey explained to them, "The demon is very cunning and is capable of many transformations. I want to catch it unawares, and that is why I didn't tell Pigsy."

Out of the cave and somersaulting through the clouds, Monkey headed straight for the demons' cave to rescue his master.

There was a great bustle in the demons' brightly candle-lit cave.
The White-Bone Demon ordered Wolf to go to Golden Light Cave
and invite her mother, Golden Toad Fairy, to come and partake
of the monk Hsuan-tsang's flesh.

Just then Bear Monster, who was on duty that day, came to the cave
with Pigsy in bonds. On his way back to rescue his master, Pigsy
had run into Bear Monster and been captured in a tussle with him.

The White-Bone Demon was very pleased and ordered her followers to bring in Hsuan-tsang and Sandy. Her mouth was watering at the prospect of the feast when she and her mother would devour their three captives.

In tears, Pigsy told Hsuan-tsang of his trip to Flower and Fruit Mountain. "Monkey said since you are kindhearted," Pigsy related, "you ought to be able to persuade the demon to set you free."

Hsuan-tsang said nothing when the demons burst into peals of
laughter at his naivety. They congratulated themselves on Monkey's refusal to leave his mountain. Just then a little goblin came
in to announce the arrival of the old Golden Toad Fairy.

The demons ushered the old fairy into the cave and offered her the
seat of honour. She grinned when she saw the three prisoners.

The White-Bone Demon ordered some goblins to kill the three.
But, with a wave of her hand, the old woman said, "Take your time!"

"I'd like to take a close look at Hsuan-tsang and see what kind of
person he is," she said. "I can't eat his flesh without knowing
what I'm eating." She walked up to the monk and, narrowing her
eyes, asked, "Are you Hsuan-tsang? How many disciples do you
have?"

Without waiting for Hsuan-tsang to answer, Sandy burst out, "Quit babbling. Go ahead and kill us!" And he gave the old fairy a kick that sent her staggering.

The White-Bone Demon rushed up to help her mother, telling her that Sandy was Hsuan-tsang's third disciple. The old woman laughed. "You're loyal all right, Sandy."

The old fairy demon glanced at Pigsy and asked the monk where his
first disciple was. The monk sighed. "He killed three people in
a single day, so at Buddha's will I sent him away."

The White-Bone Demon laughed and said to her mother, "The monk's no wiser even in the face of death. I've played him off against his first disciple." The elder demon asked, "How did you manage it, that they didn't see through your method?"

"If you don't believe me, I'll show you!" said the White-Bone Demon smugly. Then, in a twinkling she disappeared, and before the old demon stood a young girl with a basketful of steamed buns in her hand.

Smiling sweetly, she walked up to Pigsy. "Little priest," she entreated, "won't you come with me to the temple and have a bite?" Pigsy was angry and reproached himself for failing to see through a demon.

The girl vanished, and in a trice an old woman hobbled over with a stick and demanded, "Why did you kill my daughter?" The monk gave a little cry and stood there, dazed.

The old woman screeched with delight. Then, suddenly an old man appeared before the monk. "Thank you, venerable priest, for saving my life," he said.

The monk awoke as if from a dream. "You demon, why did you deceive me again and again?" he asked angrily. The old man demon laughed and replied that it was because he wanted to eat his flesh.

Sandy could stand no more and started cursing the demon. Still it was a pity that his master had been so unwise. The old man swung his stick, changing himself back into the White-Bone Demon.

"Then where did Buddha's heavenly edict come from?" asked Hsuan-
tsang in bewilderment. The demon produced the strip of yellow
silk with which it had got the monk to send Monkey away.

The monk pleaded that since he saved the demon's life three times they should be set free. "Compassion is dear to you," the old fairy demon sniffed, "but human flesh is what we want. You're crazy if you think you can talk a demon into performing charitable deeds!"

Knowing he was doomed, the monk cried out in regret, "Monkey, I shouldn't have sent you away!" Then suddenly the old fairy demon announced loudly that Monkey was there.

It was like a bolt from the blue. The old Golden Toad Fairy vanished and in her place stood Monkey, big as life. He came down on the White-Bone Demon with his staff.

The White-Bone Demon and gang scurried about looking for their weapons. At Monkey's magic sign, more monkeys appeared, and they released Hsuan-tsang and the two others.

The monkey guards escorted Hsuan-tsang out of the cave, while Pigsy and Sandy joined Monkey in the fight.

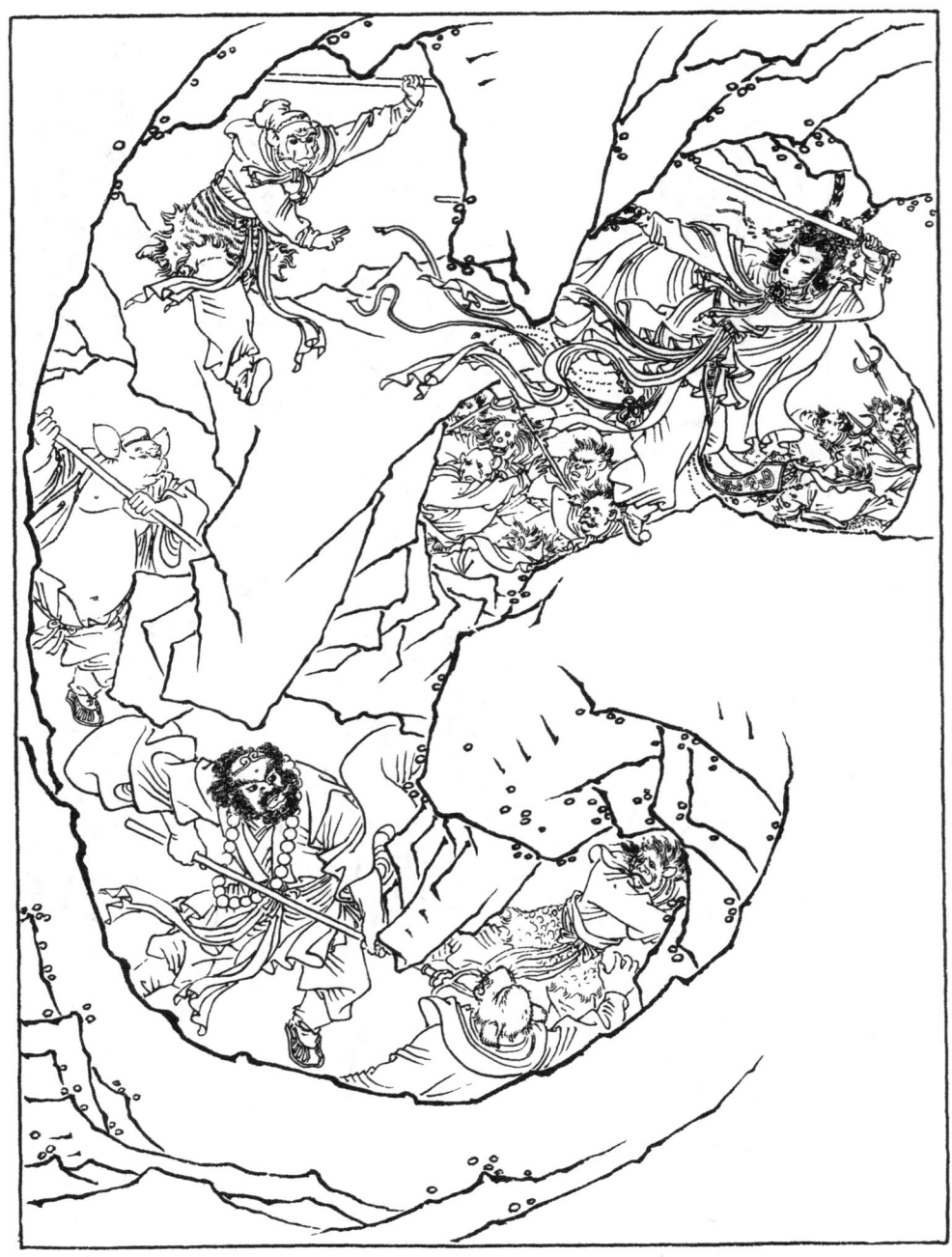

The three fought fiercely and put the demons to desperate flight.

Once out of the cave, the White-Bone Demon was about to assume
another guise when Monkey rushed up and finished her off with one
blow.   The other demons didn't last long either.

When Monkey met Hsuan-tsang, the monk felt very sorry. "How did you get back?" he asked. Monkey told how he had encountered the old Golden Toad Fairy and how he had killed her and taken her form.

Pigsy chuckled and congratulated Monkey heartily on conquering the White-Bone Demon. Monkey nodded and said, "You can't take pity on a demon!"

It was bright now, and the monk was eager to press on. So, with Monkey leading the way, the four resumed their journey westward.